# The Beast of Crowsfoot Cottage

Jean Willis was born in St Albans, Hertfordshire, in the UK. She wrote her first book when she was five. At the age of nine she produced a weekly comic called *Quimbi* for neighbours' children, with her sister who illustrated the stories.

Jeanne had her first picture book published when she was twenty-one and has now written over fifty books, including poetry and novels. She has also done loads of different jobs including selling cowboy boots, assisting a vet for reptiles and being a painter's mate. She is married with two children and lives in north London with two cats and a very old toad.

SHOCK SHOP

# The Beast
# of Crowsfoot
# Cottage

Jeanne Willis

*Illustrated by Chris Mould*

MACMILLAN CHILDREN'S BOOKS

First published 2003 by Macmillan Children's Books
a division of Macmillan Publishers Limited
20 New Wharf Road, London N1 9RR
Basingstoke and Oxford
www.panmacmillan.com

Associated companies throughout the world

ISBN 0 330 41569 7

Text copyright © Jeanne Willis 2003
Illustrations copyright © Chris Mould 2003

3 5 7 9 8 6 4 2

A CIP catalogue record for this book is available from
the British Library.

Printed and bound in Great Britain by Mackays of Chatham plc, Kent

*For Dr Peter Willis*
J.W.

# Chapter 1

I don't believe half the stuff I read in the papers, do you? I'm sure the journalists who write the articles exaggerate things. I bet if there are no really juicy stories, they just make them up to fill the pages.

I could never do that. My mum always told me it was wrong to tell lies. People should know the truth, she said, no matter how painful it is. Which is why I have to tell you what really happened to the little girl who went missing from Crowsfoot Cottage one bitterly cold winter, five years ago.

It all started with a front-page headline in our local paper, *The Bewley Herald*. If you don't live near Bewley, you won't have heard about it, so I'll put you in the picture. It said:

THE BEWLEY HERALD
Shepherd Finds Saucer-Sized Paw Print on Crowsfoot Hill

When I first read it, I laughed. Here we go again, more silly stories. Paw prints the size of saucers? Were they seriously trying to suggest there was a wild beast on the loose only a short walk from where I lived?

True, we lived right in the middle of the countryside. There was plenty of wildlife about – foxes, rabbits, owls and deer, even mink. But the only thing with big paws was Bullet, the butcher's dog, and he never went for long walks – he was too fat and he had a bad hip.

I didn't believe the story for one minute. Not until I saw the photograph. It was in black and white and clearly showed a huge paw print pressed deep into the mud. It had been raining, so the ground was very soft. I could even see the feathery lines in the soil left by the creature's fur.

You could tell the foot was huge because there was a fresh paw print of the shepherd's dog right next to it that looked tiny in comparison. The giant one could have been faked, I suppose, but I've known that shepherd since I was four. His name is Abel Crowther and his family has farmed sheep on Crowsfoot Hill for over a century. Abel is a thoughtful, serious man, not the sort who would make something up.

I cut the article out, stuck it in my scrapbook and began to wonder if there might be some truth in the tale after all.

Nothing else of any interest happened for a while. I was busy at school during the week and because of the way things were, I spent the rest of the time cooking, cleaning and shopping as usual. I never had friends round to play. There was a girl about my age who lived nearby. She seemed very nice, but she wasn't allowed to come to our cottage and I was never asked round to hers.

The following week – it must have been a Thursday – we'd run out of bread. So, to avoid trouble, as soon as I got home from school I went straight back out on my bike to fetch a loaf from the village.

I didn't mind going usually but I was really

tired that afternoon and the village is at least an hour's ride away. I'd been up late the night before, chopping wood. It was dark by the time I'd finished stacking it all in the shed, but it had to be done. Winter was coming, there was no central heating and I only had a thin blanket. I thought I was going to freeze to death sometimes.

There was a steep hill up to the baker's. I was puffed out by the time I got there. Luckily there was a customer in front of me, which gave me a chance to get my breath back.

Mrs Gledhill ran the bakery. She was serving doughnuts to an old lady called Dolly Evans. I couldn't help overhearing their conversation.

"You heard what happened to Mrs Rudge, have you, Doll?"

"Vera Rudge, d'you mean? Not passed away, has she?"

"No, dear. She was half scared to death, though. Apparently, she was stalked by a horrible wolf-like animal while she was walking her little terrier down by the old railway line."

"*What?* When?"

It was impossible, surely? Wolves have been extinct in this country for hundreds of years. It was probably just a stray dog.

"It definitely wasn't a dog," Mrs Gledhill insisted, as if she'd heard my thoughts. "Vera knows a dog when she sees one. Her father ran the kennels in Marshley, didn't he?"

Neither Mrs Rudge nor her dog had been attacked, but she was so spooked by the incident, she'd put her house up for sale and was going to live with her sister in London. It was all in the paper. Mrs Gledhill had read every word.

"Yes, dear. What can I get you?"

I'd completely forgotten what I'd come in for by then.

"A small sliced white, is it, as usual? Ooh, that's an awful black eye you've got, dear.

6

That's a real shiner.
How ever did you
do that?"

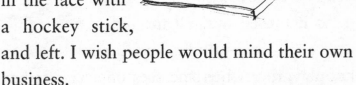

She was peering
at me suspiciously.
I told her I got hit
in the face with
a hockey stick,
and left. I wish people would mind their own
business.

There was some change left over but I knew
if I spent it, I'd be in big trouble. I never got
pocket money, so I couldn't buy anything for
myself. Not even sweets or comics. I knew it
wouldn't be like that for ever though. Mum
left me some money in her will for when I'm
eighteen.

I never did get to read the article about Mrs
Rudge and the weird wolf. Our papers hadn't
been delivered, yet again. The paperboy was
useless. He reckoned it was too far to pedal to
our cottage from the newsagent. What a

weed! He had a flashy
mountain bike with
loads of gears. I
had to do the
same journey on
my rickety old
heap every day.

As it turned out, all the kids
at school were talking about Mrs Rudge in
the playground the next day.

"Did you hear about that old dear who was
eaten by that wolf?"

"She was never eaten!"

"Oh, yeah? My brother said it bit her face
right off. He reckons it was a werewolf! It's
probably still lurking under the bridge down
by the old railway."

The railway was disused. The track was
still there but it was completely overgrown
and neglected. People used it as a dumping
ground to get rid of old mattresses, freezers
and prams. It was overrun with rats. There

was a narrow footpath nearby. Not a proper path, just a track in the grass worn down to soil, stones and roots by people walking their dogs. It was overhung by trees and there were no street lights – just the moon, if you were lucky. I always found it a peaceful place, but none of the parents at school let their children play there at night. They all wanted to go there now, of course, for a dare, but they had no chance. Not with the wolf about. Or the werewolf!

I thought the werewolf theory was a load of rubbish. The animal that followed Mrs Rudge was probably the same creature that left its paw print on Crowsfoot Hill – in which case it couldn't have been a wolf. Wolves belong to the dog family and dog paw prints always show claw marks.

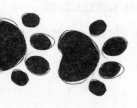

They can't retract their claws, you see. The print Abel Crowther found had no claw marks at all.

I know a lot about animals. I used to have a beautiful set of animal encyclopedias. Mum bought them for me, but they had to be torn up and thrown on the fire when we ran out of wood. It broke my heart at the time, but never mind – tough as old boots, me! At least I was allowed to borrow books from the school library.

After the wolf episode, I tried to find out everything I could about paw prints. There wasn't much in any of the books so the librarian said I could go on her computer for a little while during wet play. I was supposed to stay in the classroom really, but she was always very kind to me.

I was amazed how much information there was on the Internet. I discovered there had been hundreds of sightings of unknown species in Britain over the years. Beasts of one description or another had been seen all over the country – Inverness, Essex, Hertfordshire, Yorkshire, Warwickshire . . . everywhere. They'd been seen, but no one had ever caught one.

Some people swore they were phantoms – huge, black ghostly dogs that followed people home late at night. They were first recorded as far back as the Victorian times and were thought to be evil omens, harbingers of death.

The idea of the black dogs petrified me. I believe there is an afterlife. I have to, because one day I want to be with Mum again. But if

there is a spirit world, maybe it isn't just home to the angels. Maybe there are slobbering, phantom hounds with paw prints the size of saucers howling at the gates.

I shuddered and scrolled down. It got more and more interesting.

*Experts believe that some of the sightings could be a new strain of big cat – possibly a cross between a Scottish wild cat and an abandoned puma . . .*
*In the late sixties and early seventies it was all the rage to keep exotic cats as pets . . . until they got too big, and too hungry, perhaps.*

I knew that there were enough rabbits and birds for a large carnivore to survive on in the country. In the city, the dustbins were easy pickings. Tigers could survive on take-aways, just like urban foxes do.

In 1982, there was a creature called the

Exmoor Beast who was supposed to have killed over 200 sheep. In the end, the farmers were so desperate, they called in the Royal Marines to try to catch it. They even bought special equipment that allowed them to see and shoot in the dark, but the beast was never captured. Not on film. Not in a trap. It was far too cunning.

The school bell went for the end of play. I had just found a really good site about animal tracks when the librarian told me I'd better leave. She was sorry, but she didn't want me to be late for the next lesson and get in trouble with my teacher.

At least I managed to find out that all big cats (except cheetahs) walk with their claws pulled in, which means their paw prints look nothing like dogs' ones. I'm glad I learned that, because the next time the paper boy actually bothered to deliver the paper, I could tell that the front-page headline was barking up the wrong tree.

# DELIVERY MAN DISTURBS KILLER CHINESE FIGHTING DOG IN CROWSFOOT LANE

The beast had left more of the same paw prints as last time. They were a bit blurred, but there were *no* claw marks.

The RSPCA was called out to come and find the animal. I heard their van and their loudhailer. *"Everybody get back indoors. Stay in your houses!"*

I saw the men in uniforms running across the fields with nets and traps and guns but whatever it was had vanished.

Believe me, it was no Chinese fighting dog. I heard it roar.

# Chapter 2

Two weeks later, I dreamed I was lying at the bottom of a deep, dank hole in the middle of a field. It was dawn. Above me was a patch of gold sky the texture of fur. I wished I could pull it down into the hole and wrap it round me like a blanket. I was trembling with cold. I reached up. My arm grew longer and longer. I could hear the bones crack and the muscles tear but it didn't hurt. I brushed the sky with my fingertips and lost sight of my hand. It was as if I'd slipped it into a pocket in the clouds. My hand began to thaw. The pleasant tingling was instantly replaced by a jabbing sensation. It was getting worse. I could feel my flesh being nipped and split with scissor-like stabs and cuts. I rolled my hand over to avoid the pain, and something greasy and heavy flopped on to my palm. I couldn't shake it off – it had wrapped its bony feet round me like a handcuff. I dragged my arm back down into the hole and with it came a writhing ball of stinking black crow's feathers and a bloody beak.

More crows came. And more. The sky was clotted with them, wheeling and cursing and cawing. A gun fired and I woke up. Or did I? I could still hear the *rat-at-at* of a gun.

I shook my head. It wasn't a gun – there was some-one banging on the door.

I looked at my watch. It was very early. Barely light. Who could be calling at this time of the morning? No one else was in the

house, so I pulled my dressing gown on and called out.

"Wh . . . who is it?"

"It's the postman."

I didn't recognize his voice. Maybe it was a new postman. Or maybe it was a murderer. I wasn't going to answer the door, just in case.

"If it's a parcel, just leave it on the step," I called.

He banged urgently on the door with his fist. "Please – open this door!"

He sounded anxious, but he could have been bluffing.

"No! How do I know you're really a postman?"

"I'll show you my badge. I've got a sack full of letters. Quick!"

I opened the door a crack. He barged his way in and slammed it shut. He was breathing heavily, as if he'd been running.

"What's the matter?" I cried. "What do you want?"

He went over to the window and pulled back the curtain with a trembling hand.

"It's out there," he whispered. "In the meadow."

"*What* is?"

"The Beast!"

He slumped into the rocking chair. "The crows were mobbing it. Didn't you hear them?"

The room was so cold, his breath formed clouds as he spoke. I was used to it, but he was hugging himself to try to keep warm. I think he was in shock. I made up the fire and told him about my crow dream.

"That's nothing," he said. "I tell you, this Beast is a living nightmare. No one's safe as long as it's around. Can I use your phone?"

"There isn't one."

He stared at me in disbelief. "But this is an emergency! I have to call the police!"

There was a public phone box at the top of the lane, but he seemed very reluctant to go back outside.

"That thing is going to kill someone soon. Where's your mum and dad? You're not staying here on your own, I take it?"

"No."

The old postman knew my situation. I couldn't be bothered to explain it all over again to this new one. Instead, I asked him what the Beast looked like. I was anxious to know. The postman took his hat off and closed his eyes as if he was trying to remember every last detail.

"I had to deliver a parcel to one of the other cottages and I thought, instead of going down the lane, I'll cut across the field . . ." He shot a nervous look towards the window.

"It was pretty dark when I set off this morning, but as the sun rose, a flock of crows started to gather in the old oak tree. I remember thinking they must have found a fox kill – a rabbit or a hare, maybe."

"It could have been a deer," I said. "Foxes don't kill the deer, though. It's the poacher. He shoots them."

"Who knows what it was," he said, "But there must have been a hundred crows. Completely silent, they were, but shifty."

I've never liked crows. I hate their rolling, beady eyes and their thick black cloaks. They look as if they have been sewn together by witches.

The postman nodded. "They're sinister-looking birds. I watched them gather until

there was no room left on the branches. All of a sudden, one of them gave a signal – *craaaaak!* They all came screeching through the air like war planes aiming for the same target in the long grass."

His voice started to quaver.

"Then this thing – this great mass of fur and fangs – exploded out from under them, lashing around with claws the size of knives!" He spluttered. "The size of *carving* knives!"

"But what do you think it was?" I insisted. "A huge dog? A puma? A monster?"

He shrugged. "It all happened too fast. It had a powerful head. Enormous jaws – this wide at least."

He showed me with his hands.

"I couldn't tell the colour. It was silhouetted against the sun, so it just looked black. Then it sank back into the grass and cowered, kind of hunched up at the shoulders. And those old crows? They kept on mobbing it and attacking it until eventually it ran off."

"Which way?"

He took a deep breath.

"Towards the end of the meadow. I didn't dare move until then in case it chased me. Anyway, I picked up my postbag and hurried towards the lane. I was just making my way up to your place when I heard a low growl."

"The beast followed you here?"

He nodded.

"It was right behind me, I swear. Stalking me! I could hear it panting."

"But you didn't turn round?"

He laughed nervously. "What? And let it rip my throat out?"

I drew the curtains back. It was light. There was no sign of the Beast anywhere.

"It probably went ages ago," I told him. "Are you quite sure it wasn't a big dog? You're new around here, so you won't have met Bullet. He belongs to the butcher. He's huge – a cross between a bull terrier and a chow, I think. It would be easy to mistake him

22

for something really scary in the dark."

I knew it couldn't have been Bullet, but I didn't want the postman to hang around all day. Unfortunately, he was in no hurry to go.

Eventually, I heard the pig truck coming down the road and ran to persuade the driver to give him a lift back to the depot.

"He thinks he was followed by a wild animal," I told him. I thought the driver would laugh it off, but he didn't.

"Oh, aye? Well, you can't be too careful. Rumours are flying at the moment and there's no smoke without fire."

"What rumours?"

"I was talking to the milkman earlier," he said. "Shaking like a leaf, he was. Dropped a whole crate of gold top on account of what he saw."

"What? What did he see? Tell me!"

The driver narrowed his eyes.

"Well, I don't mean to scare you, like . . . but he did say he saw a beast with eyes the size of headlamps trying to snatch a moorhen from the village pond."

"I told you!" the postman blurted out. "I saw it in the meadow!"

The driver frowned and began to wind his window up. "I don't like the sound of it at all," he mumbled. "It'll be after my piglets next. I'd get indoors if I were you, Miss. And stay there!"

Sightings of the Beast came thick and fast after that. At first the stories were just passed on through gossip or written about in the local paper. There was a photo of the new postman standing in the meadow by the oak tree, quaking in his boots. There was another one of the milkman by the village pond, throwing bread to a moorhen. Next to it was a drawing – an artist's impression of the

Beast, drawn from the wild descriptions the locals had given him. It looked like a creature from hell.

I didn't know what to believe at the time. I was scared to go out at first, but I didn't have much choice. There was the washing to hang out on the line. There were shopping trips to the village and yet more wood to chop. I knew there was a gun in the house, just in case. Most of the country folk had them for shooting pigeons and rabbits. I wasn't sure how to use it, though, so it wasn't much comfort.

After a while, I got used to living with this new fear. Everybody did. Somehow I put the Beast to the back of my mind, concentrated on my schoolwork and tried to get on with my life.

That was until I heard a report on my portable radio one evening:

"*We have reports that Gerry Senior, the celebrity doctor who hosts the Medical Programme,* Your Very Good Health, *was involved in a serious car accident last night.*

*He was on call in the remote village of Bewley when his vehicle swerved in Crowsfoot Lane to avoid what he believed to be an escaped brown bear.*

*According to Doctor Senior, the creature, which was injured at the scene, limped off, howling, into nearby woods.*

*There have been a series of similar sightings of a large, wild animal in the area over the last few months.*

*Farmers have been advised to take extra precautions to protect their livestock, and residents have been told not to approach the animal as it may be extremely dangerous . . ."*

Until then, it had never crossed my mind that the Beast might be a bear. I've always been fond of bears. I remember thinking if it was a bear and it was starving, what choice did it have but to try to take the farmers' sheep or the village waterfowl? If it was injured, it

wouldn't be able to catch animals or birds any more. If it was in pain, it was bound to be aggressive. Even so, I prayed nobody would shoot it dead.

I had noticed a few bright spots of blood on the grass near the shed when I'd put my bike back that afternoon. The red droplets had been near to where the rabbits and gamebirds were hung, so I thought it was their blood at fter the radio report, I wasn't so sure.

I went outside and looked again. Now that the idea of an injured bear had been put into my head, I felt more concerned for its safety than my own. I wanted to rescue it. Silly, I know, but then I was only young and I knew what it was like to be alone.

I searched for paw prints the size of saucers but I didn't have any luck. The grass was covered in fallen leaves.

I was crawling around on my hands and knees when it struck me how daft I was being. Bears have great, long claws – they can't retract them like cats can. A bear would leave a paw print with unmistakable claw marks, and the prints the Beast had made had none.

It couldn't have been a bear that the doctor saw – unless, of course, it was a poor dancing bear and the owner had pulled out its claws. So what was it?

# Chapter 3

I needed to save the batteries on my little radio so I tried not to use it too often, but I was desperate for the latest news on the Beast. I tuned into the news, keeping the volume low.

I was shocked by what I heard. To be honest, I didn't know whether to laugh or cry. I felt hysterical, but I had to stay calm. Really calm. The situation had become deadly serious.

A little girl and her stepfather had gone missing in Bewley. She was the same age as me, with long, brown hair and green eyes.

She was called Sophie Ellis. I recognized the name straight away and felt sick inside. According to the news, Sophie Ellis hadn't turned up at school, which was unusual for two reasons: she had never had a day off sick in her life and no one had rung to explain her absence.

Worried that she might be ill or had been involved in a road accident, one of the teachers who lived nearby called round to see her after school. When she arrived, the cottage was in darkness but the back door was wide open. She gave an interview on the radio in a tearful voice:

*"I've known Sophie since she was in the infants'. She's a quiet, very polite child and I was worried when she didn't turn up because I knew how keen she was to help me with my book display that morning.*

*I went round to visit her on my way home to see if she was all right. There's a nasty bug going round and I thought perhaps she was ill in bed, but when I saw the back door wide open, I thought, Oh, my goodness, they've been burgled.*

*I didn't like to go in, in case the burglar was still there. I didn't have my mobile so I ran to the phone box and called 999 . . ."* At that point, her voice broke. *"If anyone has seen her, please get in touch . . ."*

The newsreader continued, *"On further investigation, the police found a trail of blood leading to a wooden outhouse a short distance from Crowsfoot Cottage. Traces of blood were also found inside the building. While there was no sign of a struggle, the incident is being treated as suspicious."*

The missing stepfather was called Briggs. I was terrified of him. He was well known in the area and no one liked him much. The landlord at the Red Lion Inn had banned him from the pub for attacking a customer with a shooting stick. He'd split the man's head open.

The Duke of Bewley, who lived in a manor house on the edge of the moor, didn't speak highly of him either, I noticed. Apparently, his gamekeeper had seen someone matching Briggs's description trying to shoot deer on his estate around dawn on the day of his disappearance.

It wasn't the first time either. In the past he'd taken pheasants out of season and laid traps to catch rabbits and hares. He was also suspected of badger baiting, but this had never been proved.

According to the police, they were looking at two theories. The first was that Briggs had murdered Sophie, disposed of her body and gone on the run. A single gunshot had been heard and traces of gunpowder had been found but no weapon and everybody knew that he didn't care much for his stepdaughter. There were dark rumours about how he treated her.

The second theory was that both stepfather and daughter had become the first human victims of the Beast.

The police couldn't say for sure until tests had been done on the blood samples. In the meantime, the public were reassured that everything was being done to track the killer down. There was a number to call if anyone had information on the missing couple. I was tempted to write it down but I didn't have a pencil on me.

I turned my radio off, curled up and went to sleep, wondering if they would ever find Sophie. The police would probably comb the countryside for her. The villagers might even join in.

It wouldn't be an easy task. There were so many places to hide a child. The forest was deep. There were caves in the hills that no one knew about except the animals. There were tunnels underground. Lots of children who go missing are never found.

I was glad that the teacher who gave the interview sounded so fond of Sophie. It was nice to know she had a friend who cared about her. All the same, I hoped the lady wouldn't worry too much. It was upsetting hearing a grown-up sob like that. If only she realized how good kids are at looking after themselves if they have to. I wish I could have told her that and put her mind at rest.

The next morning, it was snowing. I wasn't surprised. I had smelled it in the air the afternoon before. It's the one thing I will always love about England. Some people who live in hot countries have never seen snow. In Africa, the children will never know the excitement of waking up to find the countryside iced like a cake with a thick coat of blinding white, crunchy flakes.

After a fresh fall, everything looks so clean and tidy. I got up at five o'clock the next morning and played in the snow. There was no one around. I was free to yell and laugh and be happy – I even made a snow *Beast* instead of a snowman.

Afterwards, I felt guilty for enjoying myself because of the Sophie business, but life goes on – you have to grab your happiness where you can.

I had just finished my breakfast when the first police helicopter flew overhead. I didn't see it but I heard the distant throb of the whirring blades growing louder and louder. It's a threatening sound, even when you know it's someone coming to the rescue. It still makes me panic every time I think of it.

When it was right overhead, I crouched down and clamped my hands over my ears – I couldn't help it, the noise was deafening. The pilot must have been flying very low, searching the forest, the meadow and the moors.

It was a big area to cover. Weather conditions were bad. If anyone or anything had left any tracks, they would have been rubbed out by falling snow. Half an hour later, a second

helicopter came and joined the first one. They circled and buzzed over the whole of Bewley, but they had no luck. By midday, they went back to base.

All was quiet. I relaxed, made a fire and dried my wet shoes. I realized at this point that we were running out of food. It didn't matter about bread so much, but I'd probably be skinned alive if I didn't get some meat sooner or later.

I didn't want to go to the butcher in the village. The place would be swarming with police, conducting enquiries to see if they could get any leads on the missing couple. I didn't want to get mixed up in all that.

They'd want to know who was the last person to see Sophie Ellis alive. No doubt they asked Mrs Gledhill and the man in the newsagent's. "Have you seen this child before? Long brown hair and green eyes?" They would have shown them her smiling school photograph to jog their memories. That's what they usually do in these cases.

There would have been posters pinned to trees. People were forever pinning notices to the trees around the village. Usually it was to announce they had fruit and vegetables to sell. Or manure. Or that their dog had gone missing.

This time, there would be a photo of Sophie

and horrible old Briggs wrapped in a plastic
bag to protect it from the weather.

I wondered what the latest gossip was
about the Beast. Had they decided in their
hearts that he was guilty of the killings or did
they think the real beast was Briggs? I had
already made my mind up.

It was too early for the news programme, so
I went for a brisk walk to see if I could find
some fresh meat for our dinner elsewhere. I
wasn't sure what to have really. Beef was out of
the question and there was no lamb available.

There were some frozen birds but there wasn't much flesh on them. Luckily, I spotted a lovely, fat pheasant which I plucked and cooked with wild chestnuts. It was a bit tough for me, but then I'm fussy.

After dinner, I settled down and turned my radio on. I remember I had terrible indigestion, which was made even worse by the latest news item:

*"And finally tonight, there is still no sign of missing schoolgirl, Sophie Ellis, or her step-father, Keith Briggs. The search has been seriously hampered by the weather, with police helicopters grounded for much of the day because of snow.*

*House-to-house enquiries have shed no light on their disappearance, but forensic scientists have now identified blood samples found in the missing pair's outhouse.*

*I have Chief Inspector Clive Hutchins on the line. Chief Inspector Hutchins, what can* you tell us about the blood samples?"

"Good evening, Bob. There have been some interesting developments. We now have conclusive evidence that there were actually two types of blood found at the scene, one of which matched that of Keith Briggs."

"And the other type? Does it belong to the missing girl?"

"No, Bob. It does not. I can say that without a doubt. The other sample tested was not Sophie's. In fact, it was not human."

"Not *human*?"

"That is correct. We're not one hundred per cent sure what species it belongs to right now, but London Zoo is helping us with our enquiries."

"Do you think we are looking at a murder case?"

"I'm not ruling anything out at this stage but I think what we might be looking at here is an attack by a highly dangerous wild animal."

"The so-called Beast of Crowsfoot Cottage?"

"*I think so. We already have trappers on the moors around the cottage. We are now bringing in the army and flying in profession-al hunters from Canada to help capture the beast. My only fear is that it is too late for Sophie and her stepfather. The worst-case scenario is that they have both been eaten alive.*"

I shuddered. I'd hate to be eaten alive. What a dreadful way to go. Still, it wasn't definite that Sophie was dead. They hadn't found her body or her blood. Maybe they thought the Beast had dragged her off and eaten her in its lair.

I wondered how long it would take London Zoo to find out what kind of creature it really was. Not knowing was the scary part for most people, I suppose.

The radio started to fade, so I turned it off. I knew I'd have to get some more batteries soon or I wouldn't know what was going on. The paper boy wasn't about to deliver, and I could hardly catch the news on the television. We didn't have one. But then we've never had one.

I hadn't realized the trappers were already up on the moors. I decided to keep well away from there.

Before long, the place was crawling with men in camouflage gear, all on the lookout, with guns. I can't say I was impressed.

The funny thing is, I saw them, but they didn't see me!

# Chapter 4

It's incredible how quickly people forget. I noticed it first when my mum died. Six months later, when I was still red raw with sadness, other people had forgotten why I was so unhappy.

They seemed surprised and shocked to catch me still grieving. To them, my mother had died long ago. To me, it seemed like yesterday. It still does.

The second time I noticed how soon someone can disappear from public memory was shortly after Sophie Ellis went missing. I say shortly – it may have been a few weeks – I can't remember exactly. All I can tell you is that in no time at all, despite the fact that she might have been brutally murdered, she was yesterday's news. She was no longer at the front of people's minds. They let her picture fade, because she wasn't their child. Soon, they forgot their terror and let their own, beloved children play in the woods again.

By then, London Zoo had decided the blood tests they'd done on the samples taken from the shed were "inconclusive". It was animal blood, all right, but they couldn't tell what kind. The sample wasn't good enough.

If there had been a human body to examine, they would have had a better clue. Different animals kill in different ways, leaving their own trademark – a particular pattern of bites or bruises on the corpse. Bears don't actually kill with a suffocating hug, for example, they usually break the victim's neck with a massive blow from their paw. They can easily kill an ox that way. If they attack a person, they tend to use their fangs and bite the head off. A dog will go for the throat on a man, whereas some of the big cats prefer to disembowel their prey, then finish it off with a killing bite.

Sophie was still missing, presumed dead, but no one could honestly say how she died. Briggs seemed to have vanished into thin air. There had been no sign of the Beast either, but whether it had died of its injuries or simply gone underground, no one knew.

The mayor of Bewley put up a reward of five thousand pounds for anyone who managed to capture it. It was a grand gesture, but it makes me angry to this day to think that no one offered any money to find Sophie.

For a while there was a flurry of activity. Local lads who fancied their chances at outwitting the Beast went out in gangs when it grew dark, armed to the teeth. Shots were fired in the forest, but they never saw their quarry.

Once, they thought they did. They must have seen a pair of gleaming yellow eyes and

thought they'd cornered it as it crouched, ready to spring.

They aimed and fired. Unfortunately, they hit a stray goat. When they realized what they'd done, they panicked, hid the carcass under some brambles and ran away. If the farmer found out, he'd have had them arrested.

The goat didn't go to waste. When two of the lads had plucked up the courage to come back the next night to bury it, it had been eaten – bones and all. All that remained were the hooves, the horns and a hank of hair.

The army did no better. After a week of churning the countryside into mud with their heavy boots they were recalled. They were needed elsewhere.

The Canadian hunters found no evidence at all. They dug a big hole and made an elaborate trap baited with a dead sheep. You could smell it for miles. They hid up trees with binoculars for hours. They collected dung. They searched the undergrowth and found . . . nothing.

They were about to give up and go home when one of Abel's prize rams was attacked and killed. I heard them discussing it on their walkie-talkies.

Later, the Canadians made a public announcement. They said that Abel Crowther's ram had been savaged by a large, domestic dog of some kind, probably a mastiff, judging by the teeth marks. All the signs of a dog-kill were there, they insisted.

There was no bear, no big cat. If there had been, they'd have found it. That was their job and they were the best in the business, or so they reckoned. They'd tracked every kind of animal worldwide – tigers, mountain lions, gorillas and grizzlies – but all they found here were the usual British mammals.

In their experience, dog prints swell like anything when the ground is boggy. The paw print the size of a saucer was a hoax. The hunters were going back to Canada. Case closed.

There were no more sightings of the Beast that winter, as far as I know. I began to relax. For a while, although things were tough, it was a peaceful, happy time for me.

It wasn't until early spring that the whole business started up again.

Three boys had pitched a tent in a field about five miles west of Bewley. When I found out, I remember thinking they couldn't have been in the Scouts, because the Scouts always use an official campsite further south, which has running water, proper facilities and even a cookhouse.

This field was in the middle of nowhere. The tent was small. It was the old-fashioned, no-frills variety made of khaki

canvas with a loose tie-front, staked out with metal pegs.

Anyway, by all accounts these boys had escaped from Ridgley Park, a boarding school for juvenile delinquents – boys who had been in trouble with the law but were too young to be sent to prison. Ridgley Park is notorious for its cruel masters and strict regime. Once, a boy of nine had been made to clean the toilets with his toothbrush for talking in class. Another had been made to stand out in the snow in his pyjamas for flicking peas during dinner. Little wonder the inmates were so desperate to leave.

It was hardly the time of year to be living in a tent. Although the days were getting warmer, I knew from experience that the nights were bitterly cold.

The boys were used to certain hardships, but not these conditions. They were from the city. They were tough, but they didn't have the skills or the equipment to survive in the country for more than a few days.

For a start, they had pitched their tent in a ditch. When it rained, the ditch would fill with water, like a bath, and they would get soaked. They had no spare clothes. All they had were the ones they ran off in, and a radio, a lighter, a kettle, a few tins of food and some fruit they'd stolen from the Ridgley canteen.

I'm not sure how long they would have lasted in that tent if they hadn't had the shock of their lives and run screaming back to where they'd come from. They would probably have died from exposure, but they never got the chance.

What happened was this. It was dawn. As the sun rose, a thick, yellow mist hung over the fields and there was a moaning wind. The three boys were still asleep, huddled together for warmth.

They had tried to make a fire the night before, but the firewood they had gathered was too green and too damp and they didn't know what they were doing. They had opened some tins of corned beef, hoping to cook the meat into a warming hash, perhaps. However, they had given up, eaten their fruit instead and gone to bed bad-tempered and hungry. As they slept, the faint smell of fatty meat hung in the air.

Something woke one of the boys. A snuffling sound. A fox, maybe? He froze. He knew little about foxes. Were they fierce? Did they attack humans?

There was a low, deep growl. Suddenly, a huge, furry paw thrust itself into the tent between the ground sheet and the grass. It began to feel around, then one of its long claws must have got caught in a blanket thread, because slowly . . . slowly . . . the blanket was dragged off the three boys.

The one who was awake watched helplessly as it was pulled out through the gap under the tent. Now the other two woke up, exposed to the sudden cold, and in their sleepy confusion, accused the third boy of stealing the blanket.

Pale and trembling, he pointed his finger as the corner of the blanket finally slipped under the tent, punctuated by irritated growls and thumps from outside.

Imagine their terror as the massive silhouette of the Beast's shaggy head loomed closer and closer and their curdling screams as it burst through the tent flap and roared.

Somehow, those boys got away. Somehow, they shuffled through the back end of the tent, pulling out two of the guy ropes as they did so. As the tent collapsed on top of the Beast, they raced blindly down the field, splashed through a foul ditch and ran all the way back to the relative comfort of Ridgley Park where they told their story to anyone foolish enough to believe them.

The headmaster did. After all, what could possibly have made three hooligan boys who had been so keen to escape so very glad to return? Something must have put the wind up them.

The story didn't make the national headlines. Perhaps the broadcasters didn't believe in the Beast or the boys, because the item was fitted in at the last minute on the local news. I'd managed to get hold of some new batteries by then, so I was able to listen to the whole thing clearly.

The police were called and the field

searched. They found the tent. It originally belonged to a Mr Mitchell, the caretaker at Ridgley Park – the boys had stolen it from his hut the day they escaped across the roof and slid down the drainpipe to freedom.

Mr Mitchell had been keen to have his tent back – he was fond of camping – but it was useless to him now. It was ripped to shreds but, as the chief inspector explained, all of the lads except one were carrying penknives and they weren't afraid to use them.

It was agreed that the rips in the tent were far more likely to be the handiwork of frustrated boys than the claws of a savage beast.

I wasn't so sure but kept my hunch to myself. After all, whoever took the opinion of a little girl seriously?

I like to think that afterwards, those three unhappy boys thought twice about running away again. I hope they served their time at Ridgley and weren't punished too harshly. I hope they went on to become good, kind people, living decent lives – so few do. I'm thinking in particular about Sophie's step-father here – wondering if he had bullied Sophie because someone had bullied him as a child. If so, should I pity him? I find it hard, knowing what I know.

I wish those Ridgley Boys well, wherever they are. I'd love to meet them and shake them by the hand. They did me a big favour, not that they'll ever know it.

Shortly after the camping incident, a bird-watcher found some empty tins of corned beef in an abandoned tree house in a forest not a million miles from where those boys had pitched their tent.

Nothing so odd in that, you may think, and nor did he at first – but then he discovered something that worried him enough to alert the authorities.

Stuffed inside the tins were several lengths of brown, human hair.

# Chapter 5

The discovery of the chopped hair in the corned beef tins caused quite a stir. The Sophie Ellis case was reopened and extra police were drafted in to make a thorough search of the forest.

They ripped the tree house apart looking for clues, but found no real evidence. Someone had certainly been living there, because they found a scorched circle of earth down below – evidence of a small wood fire which contained the remains of a few charred animal bones.

The fire could have been built by a child, but it was unlikely. The bones belonged to a goat. What was the likelihood of a young girl killing and butchering a goat?

No, this was the work of a poacher. Could it have been Briggs? Was he so twisted that he had murdered Sophie in the forest, buried her and cut off her long, brown hair to keep as a trophy?

It said on the news that they looked for signs of a small grave. They would have had their work cut out. Parts of the forest were impossible for an adult to penetrate, even if they got on their stomachs and crawled.

If the police hacked with their scythes all week, they would never have cleared the thick tangle of brambles and roots that hid a thousand secrets – birds, insects, creatures no one ever sees, going about their lives in the gloomy, green privacy of the undergrowth.

Still, I'm glad to say the police didn't give up easily, even in the pouring rain. To their credit, they didn't leave completely empty-handed.

They found one good piece of evidence – a

blood-soaked bandage half-woven into a bird's-nest in the crook of a low-hanging branch.

I'm not sure if they discovered to whom the blood belonged. I don't think they could have done. It can't have been fresh and the bandage would have been in a terrible mess if a bird had mixed it with wet mud and twigs.

Oh, I nearly forgot to mention the paw prints. They found several, just as they were leaving the forest. They were the size of saucers and led to a swollen river. They could have belonged to a large, domestic dog, but, suddenly, the police weren't so sure. They took plaster casts. I don't know how good they were because, as I said, it had been raining really hard.

I did hear later that the prints were even deeper than the ones Abel found on Crowsfoot Hill. Now, that could have been because the ground was so sloppy – or it could have been because the Beast had put on weight. Maybe he'd had a big meal the size a small girl?

The police did their best but, despite following several leads, Sophie Ellis still wasn't found and nor was Briggs.

I followed the story whenever and however I could – sometimes on my radio, sometimes from newspapers that had been thrown away. I hated to see Sophie's face crumpled up and dumped in the rubbish. She didn't look a bit like she did in real life.

The search had spread much further than Bewley now. I felt as if I couldn't get away from it. It was Easter by then – warm but windy – and as I walked along, hanging on to my hat, I thought how nice it would be to go abroad.

I'd never had a proper holiday but I'd always dreamed that, one day, I would go somewhere exotic. Now the idea appealed to me more and more. I knew we couldn't afford it. Going abroad would cost hundreds of pounds. Even so, I looked into how we might go about it, because you never know. There are ways and means if you put your mind to it.

In the past, I had my heart set on going to Russia. I don't know why. Maybe because I love the snow. Still, Russia is not to all tastes.

Now I fancied travelling somewhere hot. Somewhere with palm trees, golden sand and sea as warm as a bath. I wanted to take a friend, which was a problem, but it wasn't impossible.

I'd never been on an aeroplane and, to tell you the truth, I didn't like the idea of flying much. I love going on boats though. When Mum was alive, we went on a trip down the Thames in London and it was one of the best days of my life. I didn't feel sick at all. She told me I must have good sea legs, like my great-grandfather, Billy. He was a sailor on a clipper – a ship that sailed to the tropics, bringing back its cargo of ivory and gold. He'd run away to sea when he was fifteen.

He'd taken the train to the docks, sneaked on board a ship called the *Merry Maid* and hidden in a rum barrel. By the time they found him, it was too late to row him ashore. The captain threatened to throw him overboard, but the ship's cook took pity on him and gave him a job working in the galley.

He made a good life for himself, Mum said. He brought back treasures from around the world – hand-carved, ivory scissors from Swaziland, Indian bracelets made from hundreds of tiny glass beads, silk slippers from Thailand. He could speak several languages, too, including Swahili.

Mum taught me some. *Jambo* means Hello. *Kwenda wapi*, How are you? There were loads more. For some reason, the phrases stuck in my mind. Well, you never know when these things are going to come in useful.

Talking of boats and trains, it was during that same Easter holiday that the police were alerted to a strange incident, which may or may not have been anything to do with the missing girl.

They must have felt obliged to follow it up anyway, even if the latest story sounded like the ravings of a lunatic. A lot of money had been spent on this unsolved crime. The public expected results.

You must forgive me if I leave out some of the details of the next event. My poor old radio had just about had it by then and, apart from the occasional crackly report, I had to rely on what I saw or overheard.

I know for certain it happened on the Sunday, April the twenty-third, because it was my birthday. I'm not likely to forget that, am I?

Anyway, from what I can gather, it seems that a railway worker on a night shift disturbed a dwarf who was sleeping under a

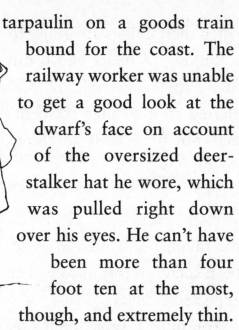

tarpaulin on a goods train bound for the coast. The railway worker was unable to get a good look at the dwarf's face on account of the oversized deerstalker hat he wore, which was pulled right down over his eyes. He can't have been more than four foot ten at the most, though, and extremely thin. His clothes and nails were filthy and he had sacks tied over his shoes, as if the soles had worn through. He had clearly been sleeping rough. He also wore a long, droopy moustache, like a Chinese mandarin, and a dark, scruffy beard.

It wasn't the first time the railway man had found a tramp snatching a quiet snooze on his train, but never before had he encountered such violence.

Having been startled out of a deep sleep, the dwarf jumped up in a fury and fumbled for a pair of ill-fitting spectacles with a smashed lens. He then whistled through his thumbs and summoned an enormous creature out of nowhere – maybe a boar hound, maybe a bear. Whatever it was gave a guttural bark and leaped on to the railway worker from behind, the force of its great paws smashing him face down on to the rails.

For a moment he felt the rough rasp of its tongue tasting his neck then, mercifully, everything went black. The blow to his forehead had knocked him out. The next thing he remembered was waking up in an ambulance, wondering where on earth he was.

Slowly, it must have come back to him because he gave an interview on the radio. I only heard a fraction of what he said, but he seemed to be making a meal of it. He only had a small gash to his forehead. If the animal that attacked him had been as fierce as he described, surely it would have ripped his throat out? I think he'd been drinking.

Never mind what I thought, people were gripped by the report. The dwarf and his demon sidekick were certainly the topic of the day. Where had they come from and who were they?

Some people thought the railway worker had been attacked by Briggs and the Beast of Crowsfoot Cottage who, in their minds, was nothing more than one of the vicious dogs he borrowed to bait badgers.

I think not. Briggs was a short man, but he was no dwarf. And if the Beast was a dog, how do they explain the paw prints the police found outside the forest – the ones they took casts of? I know paw prints swell in the mud – but that much? And there were no claw marks.

Some said the dwarf was a Chinese magician who had turned to crime and that the beast he summoned wasn't an animal but his savage accomplice who was so hideously deformed he had to be disguised in skins.

I liked that story. It was so wild, so far-fetched it truly made me laugh.

Clearly, other people didn't find it so amusing. Especially when the final witness claimed to have seen something equally strange.

It happened down at the docks the next day. It was early and the dock workers were busy loading crates on to the cargo ships.

There were several sailors hanging around on the jetty. I suppose most of them would be going to sea for several months because the ships from that dock sailed to far-flung places like the South Sea Islands, the Ivory Coast, Japan – such romantic places!

The sailors' wives and girlfriends were there, too, saying their goodbyes.

I don't know if I'd like to be a sailor's wife. They say that sailors have a girl in every port, but Mum said it wasn't true.

Great-grandfather Billy only ever had eyes

for one woman, and that was my great-
grandmother, Kathleen. They seem to have
had a very happy marriage, despite Great-
grandma being on her own most of the time.
If she could cope with it, I know I could. I've
had plenty of practice surviving without
human company. Who needs it?

Where was I? Ah yes, sailors' wives. They
are an important part of this story – at least

one of them is. Her name is Amanda, and she was saying goodbye to her man and she was sobbing. I was sorry to hear that. Goodbyes can be so hard.

She must have been crying on his shoulder because as she looked up through her tears, she suddenly exclaimed that she had seen the strangest sight – a tiny man with a droopy moustache and a great big hat had just climbed into a large wooden crate on wheels! He'd pulled the lid right down so he couldn't be seen, but the funniest thing was that, just before he closed the lid, she swore she saw a long, furry tail sticking out.

To this day, I don't know if the sailor believed her, but they say stranger things happen at sea.

# Chapter 6

If the sailor's wife was correct, that was the last sighting of the Beast in Britain. There were no more sheep ripped to pieces. No more massive paw prints. The trail had gone cold.

Had the Beast ever really existed? Or were the shepherd, the milkman, the postman and all the others who claimed to have seen it either mad or the most fantastic liars?

Little Sophie Ellis was never found and I hope she never will be. It has been five years since she went missing and I think she should be left in peace now. Her mother would have wanted that.

I still find it very hard to talk about Briggs. You will have gathered by now that he was a cruel man, but you don't know the half of it. If you knew what he had done to Sophie, you would want to kill him. You would be too late though. He is already dead.

Yes, Briggs is dead. I'm still not sure how I feel about that. He was a man who enjoyed watching badgers being torn apart by his hounds. He left rabbits to scream in the wire snares he'd hidden near their burrows. Everybody knew that he made Sophie's life a living hell – I should be delighted that he's gone.

Yet I feel guilty. Goodness knows why. Maybe we all feel a little bit guilty when someone dies, especially if that person dies suddenly and in such a harrowing way.

Do I believe Briggs was murdered? I did at first. But now I am convinced that what happened between Briggs and Sophie was an accident.

He was killed in the shed by a single shot from his own gun. The bullet went straight through his left eye and through an old hole in the back wall where a knot of wood had fallen out. I suppose the bullet got lost in the shrubbery. Or it may have plopped down the water well. No one ever found it.

Briggs died instantly. In a way I wish he hadn't. He might have liked the chance to say sorry for his sins as he lay dying but it was all over too quickly. Bang! He was gone.

Just a short while earlier, he must have come back feeling pretty good about himself. He'd been poaching on the duke's estate and although he hadn't managed to bag himself a deer, he'd caught a couple of fat rabbits and managed to give the gamekeeper the slip yet again.

After he'd hung the rabbits up, he'd gone inside to have his breakfast. He had a huge appetite and his stepdaughter cooked for him every day – only this time there was no smell of bacon and no sign of the cook.

This would certainly have put him in a foul

mood, but no matter how he yelled and hollered, Sophie didn't appear. Not this time.

She hadn't overslept. The fire hadn't been made. Her bicycle was still there so she couldn't have gone to school. Where was she?

With the gun still in his hand, he searched for her outside. She wasn't hanging out the washing or sweeping the yard or chopping wood. There was a low whining noise coming from the outhouse, like a creature in pain. Or a girl sobbing? Briggs walked silently and furiously across the grass towards it and stared through the thick, yellow cobwebs that hung like a torn lace curtain across the small window.

I will leave you to imagine the look of terror on his face when he saw that the

Beast was inside the shed. Once he'd got over the initial shock, his fear turned to bloodlust and he sidled round to the wooden door, kicked it open with his boot and raised his gun. A voice cried out.

"*No!*"

The police say there was no evidence of a struggle, but there was one.

In an heroic effort to stop him shooting the injured Beast as it lay exhausted on the shed floor, Sophie charged at her stepfather and tried to wrestle his gun away.

An oil lamp was knocked off its hook. The crop of carrots she had tended all summer and preserved in a box of sand fell off its shelf. There was a loud crack and a plume of smoke. Briggs's knees buckled and he crumpled in a heap.

People often said that Sophie Ellis was a practical girl. I wasn't sure what they meant at the time, but maybe they simply meant that she was the kind of child who, having just witnessed a horrific death, was still able to tidy up any fallen vegetables, rehang the oil lamp and stay calm.

Meanwhile, the starving beast gnawed, crunched and swallowed the pathetic remains of her stepfather. The only things it spat out were his spectacles, his boots and his hat.

In his defence, he was guilty of eating Briggs. But *not* of eating him alive. By the time the police arrived, nothing remained. The scene of the crime had been licked clean. All except for a few stubborn stains which had soaked into the wood. Most of the blood belonged to Briggs. The rest came from a deep wound on the Beast's hind leg which, despite Sophie's best efforts, continued to seep through the bandage she'd dressed it with.

The girl slipped through the shadows of trees carrying the gun. She followed the limping creature to its lair with its miles of secret tunnels under the hill. There they rested in near darkness, gathering their strength while the injured beast digested its horrible meal, its eyes shining like amber traffic lights.

The animal was lucky – it had a coat of thick, tawny fur. It couldn't feel the icy draughts that made Sophie shiver and sneeze. She knew she would die of cold if she didn't light a fire soon, so she felt her way through the maze of tunnels with the Beast as her guide, like a blind person, stopping now and then to warm her frozen hands against its breath.

They emerged, blinking at the moonlight. Although they were in the deepest part of the forest, for a moment it seemed painfully bright outside after the gloom of the tunnel.

Sophie quickly made a fire and ate some carrots. After she was warmed through, she built a tree house for them to sleep in. The Beast liked to sleep high up among the leaves. When they woke up, it was snowing. For a little while, Sophie forgot all her troubles and played in the snow until the wind got up and started to blow it into freezing drifts.

It was shortly after that the first helicopter came over. Even if it hadn't snowed, I don't think the search party would ever have found her. She knew the area better than anyone. She knew where to hide. She had spent her life hiding from Briggs and his beatings.

Now he was dead and she had befriended the Beast, I suppose it would be true to say that for the first time in her life she had nothing to fear – except being found, of course.

This sharpened her wits and made her cunning. Wherever they went, whatever they did, she tried her best to cover their tracks. It wasn't always possible but, remarkably, she got away with it.

She even watched the trappers come and go from one of their own traps! The sniffer dogs never detected her or the Beast because the stench of rotten sheep the Canadians used for bait covered their scent.

Food was hard to come by in the winter, as you can imagine. Since he was wounded, the Beast couldn't chase his own prey, so Sophie had to hunt or trap small mammals and game birds. It didn't take her long to master the gun.

She would cook a bit for herself, but she always gave him the lion's share and went hungry most of the time. Just like she did with Briggs. Finding the dead goat was a godsend – she'd roasted the flesh and lived on the remaining cold meat for days. The Beast had eaten the rest raw.

Sophie knew right from wrong and she would never steal anything under normal circumstances. There were times when she was forced to, though. When those three boys pitched their tent in the field, she took their batteries, their kettle, their lighters and all their food. You have to remember she had run out of matches by now and hadn't eaten properly for days.

At the time, she was surviving on leaf buds and mushrooms and had been searching for hours for something to eat. The corned beef had been irresistible and they'd eaten the lot.

Once spring came there had been wild birds' eggs for breakfast, but as much as Sophie loved the forest, she knew she couldn't stay there for ever. The Beast's leg was much better and it was time to move on.

Where could they go? Sophie had no desire to go home. But the Beast did. She was sure of it. She came up with a plan.

In order for it to work, she would have to travel, and travelling meant she had to risk being seen in public. Even if she managed to keep the Beast out of sight if her face was recognized, the plan would fail.

She decided to go in disguise. Using a penknife she had stolen from the Ridgley Boys' tent, she hacked off her hair almost down to the scalp. Then she made a long moustache from a few of the strands, shaped the ends with earwax and stuck this to her upper lip with some sticky tree sap. She

attached some even shorter pieces to her chin to suggest a scruffy beard.

By the time she'd put on her stepfather's chewed, old hat and shattered glasses, her own mother wouldn't have known who she was. Under the cover of darkness, she left the sanctuary of the forest, riding on the Beast's scarred back.

They headed for the nearest railway depot. The train had already been loaded when they got there, so apart from the driver and the guard who were in the hut, there was no one around to notice the two of them crawling under the tarpaulin which covered the last truck.

The train trundled down the track. Using the Beast as a pillow, Sophie fell into an exhausted sleep as they were carried hundreds of miles to the opposite end of the country.

At the docks, she was rudely awakened by a railway worker and, in her panic, she commanded the Beast to see him off. She hadn't meant the man to get hurt but, unfortunately, the Beast had been too enthusiastic and knocked him over. Sophie would tell you that the Beast was very sorry for what he'd done and tried to lick him better but the railway man, in his confusion, told a very different story to the press.

As for the sailor's wife, she saw what she saw. Sophie and the Beast climbed into an empty wooden crate and, not realizing what was inside, the docker rolled it up the gang-plank and on to the ship.

It wasn't a clipper because they don't have those any more. It was a cargo ship, carrying medical supplies to Africa. It was called the *Lucky Star*.

It was a rough crossing, particularly around the Cape of Good Hope, but Sophie was an excellent sailor. It ran in her family. Despite the cramped conditions inside the crate, she and her companion, the dreaded Beast, survived by climbing out under the cover of darkness to search for scraps left by the crew. They made it to East Africa where they hope to live out the rest of their lives in peace.

How do I know all this?

I am Sophie Ellis. I'm writing to you from our tree house in the jungle because, as I said at the beginning, my mother always told me to tell the truth.

The Beast is very old now. He'll always have a limp from that car injury but I want you to know he is happy at last. We both are.

I'm no longer a frightened little girl and although he might not look like the king of the beasts any more, he'll always be my sweet, tatty, gentle lion.

I watch him sometimes when he's sleeping. I wonder if he remembers his circus days and if he ever forgave the ringmaster who whipped him and left him to die on Crowsfoot Moor – all because the audience thought he was too tame.

I'm sure he forgave him, you know. He doesn't hate anyone. He loves people, even though one of them hurt him so badly.

One day, I hope, I'll be like him and find it in my heart to forgive Briggs.

Another book in the Shock Shop series . . .

# Hairy Bill
*Susan Price*

Something came down the chimney in Alex's bedroom in the night – something that paused and, in a Scottish accent, asked for *Mathesons*. Alex thought he was dreaming. But his mum's name is Matheson. And when he goes downstairs the next morning, something is clearly very wrong.

The house is unnaturally, indeed frighteningly, tidy. Has there been a break-in – by obsessively tidy thieves? Or is there another, more sinister explanation? Meet Hairy Bill – a Scottish supernatural whirlwind of terrifying tidiness.